Let's Go, Illini!

Aimee Aryal

Illustrated by Anuj Shrestha

MASCOT
BOOKS™

www.mascotbooks.com

It was a beautiful fall day at the University of Illinois at Urbana-Champaign.

ALMA MATER
TO THY HAPPY CHILDREN
OF THE FUTURE
THOSE OF THE PAST
SEND GREETINGS

Two little Illini fans were on their way to Memorial Stadium to watch a football game. Let's follow them to the game!

The little Illini stopped in front of the Illini Union.

Two students walking by shouted, "Let's go, Illini!"

The little Illini walked down the Quad and passed by classroom buildings.

A professor waved and said,
"Let's go, Illini!"

The little Illini passed in front of Foellinger Auditorium.

A girl standing on the echo plaque yelled, "Let's go, Illini!"

The little Illini walked by the Morrow Plots and saw the Undergraduate Library in the distance.

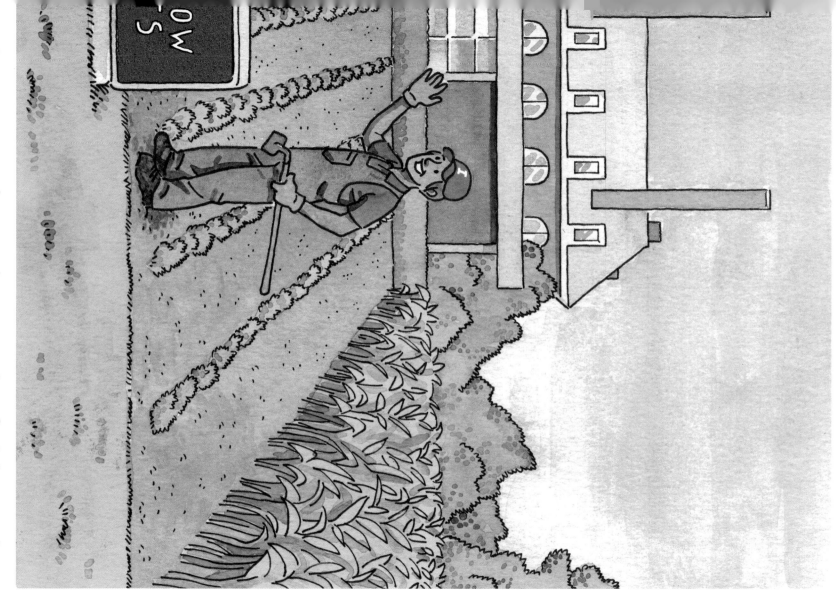

Some people working in the fields said,
"Let's go, Illini!"

The little Illini walked over to Assembly Hall where the Fighting Illini play basketball.

They ran into a basketball player and the coach outside the arena. The coach said "Let's go, Illini!"

It was almost time for the football game.
As the little Illini walked to the stadium,
they passed by some alumni.

The alumni remembered going to games when they went to U of I. They said, "Let's go, Illini!"

Finally, the little Illini arrived at Memorial Stadium. They watched the game and cheered for the team.

The Fighting Illini scored six points!
The quarterback shouted,
"Touchdown, Illini!"

At halftime the Marching Illini moved into the "Three In One" formation.

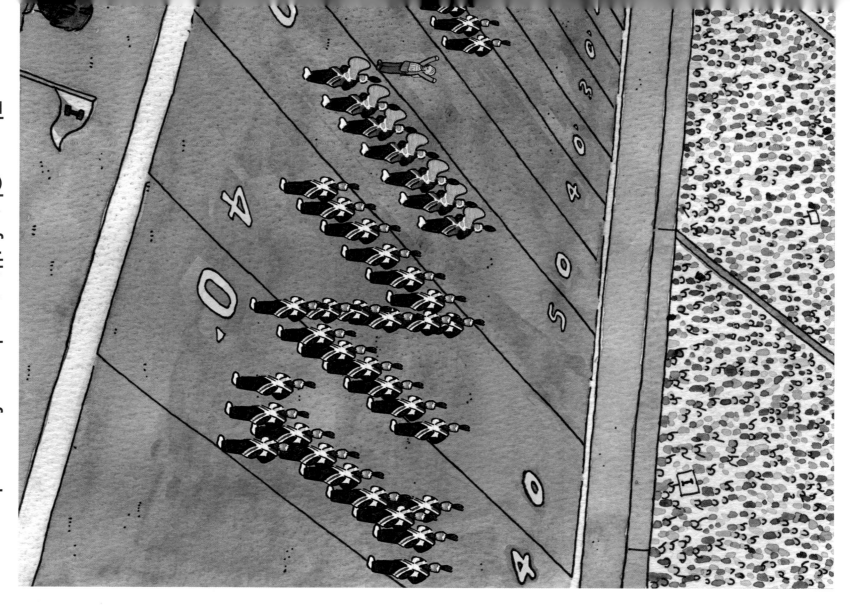

Then Chief Illiniwek performed his traditional dance. The little Illini yelled, "Let's go, Illini!"

The University of Illinois Fighting Illini won the football game!

The little Illini gave the coach
a high-five. The coach said,
"Great game, Illini!"

After the football game, the little Illini were tired. It had been a long day at the University of Illinois.

They walked to their homes and climbed into their beds.

"Goodnight, little Illini."

This one is for my Mom, Renee Kazmar Sutter, and her granddaughters, Anna and Maya. ~ AA

Dedicated to the Illini peoples and the memory of their ancestors. ~ AS

For information please contact Mascot Books, P.O. Box 220157, Chantilly, VA 20153-0157.

ISBN: 1-932888-21-7

Printed in the United States.

www.mascotbooks.com

MASCOT BOOKS
www.mascotbooks.com

MLB

Boston Red Sox
Hello, Wally!
by Jerry Remy

*Wally's Journey Through
Red Sox Nation*
by Jerry Remy

New York Yankees
Let's Go, Yankees!
by Yogi Berra

New York Mets
Hello, Mr. Met!
by Rusty Staub

St. Louis Cardinals
Hello, Fredbird!
by Ozzie Smith

Chicago Cubs
Let's Go, Cubs!
by Aimee Aryal

Chicago White Sox
Let's Go, White Sox!
by Aimee Aryal

Philadelphia Phillies
Hello, Phillie Phanatic!
by Aimee Aryal

Cleveland Indians
Hello, Slider!
by Bob Feller

More Coming Soon

NBA

Dallas Mavericks
Let's Go, Mavs!
by Mark Cuban

NFL

Dallas Cowboys
How 'Bout Them Cowboys!
by Aimee Aryal

Collegiate

Auburn University
War Eagle! by Pat Dye
Hello, Aubie! by Aimee Aryal

Boston College
Hello, Baldwin! by Aimee Aryal

Brigham Young University
Hello, Cosmo!
by Pat and LaVell Edwards

Clemson University
Hello, Tiger! by Aimee Aryal

Duke University
Hello, Blue Devil! by Aimee Aryal

Florida State University
Let's Go 'Noles! by Aimee Aryal

Georgia Tech
Hello, Buzz! by Aimee Aryal

Indiana University
Let's Go Hoosiers! by Aimee Aryal

James Madison University
Hello, Duke Dog! by Aimee Aryal

Kansas State University
Hello, Willie! by Dan Walter

Louisiana State University
Hello, Mike! by Aimee Aryal

Michigan State University
Hello, Sparty! by Aimee Aryal

Mississippi State University
Hello, Bully! by Aimee Aryal

North Carolina State University
Hello, Mr. Wuf! by Aimee Aryal

Penn State University
We Are Penn State! by Joe Paterno
Hello, Nittany Lion! by Aimee Aryal

Purdue University
Hello, Purdue Pete! by Aimee Aryal

Rutgers University
Hello, Scarlet Knight! by Aimee Aryal

Syracuse University
Hello, Otto! by Aimee Aryal

Texas A&M
Howdy, Reveille! by Aimee Aryal

UCLA
Hello, Joe Bruin! by Aimee Aryal

University of Alabama
Roll Tide! by Kenny Stabler
Hello, Big Al! by Aimee Aryal

University of Arkansas
Hello, Big Red By Aimee Aryal

University of Connecticut
Hello, Jonathan! by Aimee Aryal

University of Florida
Hello, Albert! by Aimee Aryal

University of Georgia
How 'Bout Them Dawgs!
by Vince Dooley
Hello, Hairy Dawg! by Aimee Aryal

University of Illinois
Let's Go, Illini! by Aimee Aryal

University of Iowa
Hello, Herky! by Aimee Aryal

University of Kansas
Hello, Big Jay! by Aimee Aryal

University of Kentucky
Hello, Wildcat! by Aimee Aryal

University of Maryland
Hello, Testudo! by Aimee Aryal

University of Michigan
Let's Go, Blue! by Aimee Aryal

University of Minnesota
Hello, Goldy! by Aimee Aryal

University of Mississippi
Hello, Colonel Rebel! by Aimee Aryal

University of Nebraska
Hello, Herbie Husker! by Aimee Aryal

University of North Carolina
Hello, Rameses! by Aimee Aryal

University of Notre Dame
Let's Go Irish! by Aimee Aryal

University of Oklahoma
Let's Go Sooners! by Aimee Aryal

University of South Carolina
Hello, Cocky! by Aimee Aryal

University of Southern California
Hello, Tommy Trojan! by Aimee Aryal

University of Tennessee
Hello, Smokey! by Aimee Aryal

University of Texas
Hello, Hook 'Em! by Aimee Aryal

University of Virginia
Hello, CavMan! by Aimee Aryal

University of Wisconsin
Hello, Bucky! by Aimee Aryal

Virginia Tech
Yea, It's Hokie Game Day!
by Cheryl and Frank Beamer
Hello, Hokie Bird! by Aimee Aryal

Wake Forest University
Hello, Demon Deacon!
by Aimee Aryal

West Virginia University
Hello, Mountaineer! by Aimee Aryal

NHL

Coming Soon

Visit us online at www.mascotbooks.com for a complete list of titles.